Barbara Robertson began her career as a primary school teacher in London and Hampshire. She lived and taught in Canada for many years, where she was also involved in organising community nursery schools, and taught special needs to adolescents in crisis. On returning to the UK she again taught in London before moving to County Durham. She has published two other books for children: *Moving Day* (Stockwell, 2012) and *Viking Ventures* (Book Guild, 2013).

By the same author:

Viking Ventures, Book Guild Publishing, 2013

Brindle

Barbara Robertson

Book Guild Publishing
Sussex, England

First published in Great Britain in 2013 by
The Book Guild Ltd
The Werks
45 Church Road
Hove, BN3 2BE

Printed and bound in Great Britain by
CPI Group (UK) Ltd, Croydon, CR0 4YY

A catalogue record for this book is available from
The British Library.

ISBN 978 1 84624 936 5

For family and friends

Contents

Brindle the Postman

Brindle lived with the Marsh family at Number 10 Green Trees Avenue. He was a busy little dog, a Cairn Terrier. His rough-haired coat was a dark brown mixed with black, which was why he was called Brindle; and he had a large black patch on one ear. He was very lively and mischievous and he loved to play with the two children, Rhona and Rob, who also lived at Number 10.

Mr Marsh went to work every day in a large city office and Mrs Marsh was an estate agent. She was always busy showing people houses.

When it was the weekend Brindle was very happy; there was lots to do. When Mr Marsh went to get his newspaper, Brindle would run beside him, chasing the cats and wagging his tail at anyone they would meet. If Mrs Marsh went shopping in the village he would go too,

past the duck pond and the Post Office. He would sniff at the trees and play with the other dogs they met. But he did not like being tied up outside the supermarket, he wanted to go inside and explore where the sausages were kept on the butcher's counter.

His favourite outing was football practice with Rob and Rhona. Sometimes he managed to chase the ball with

the football players; they were not always too pleased about that!

Weekends were fun with country walks, sailing boats and games of ball in the garden. There was always something good to do.

But oh, the weeks! They were so long and lonely. Everybody was out and poor Brindle spent the days at home all by himself. It was such a long day from the time when everyone left in the morning until the children came home from school to play with him and take him out for a walk. He was always so pleased to see them.

Next door at Number 12 lived Mr and Mrs Tomkins. Each morning Mr Tomkins would set off for work at about half past eight, he would walk to the bus stop and get on the bus to Grinton. Brindle used to watch him set off every morning. He would sit on the sofa and observe Mr Tomkins through a gap in the curtains. He wondered where he was going.

One morning Brindle decided to go with him, he had to be very careful that no one would see him. So he waited, hidden by the coats in the hall, until Mrs Marsh went to get the car out of the garage. Then he slipped outside into the garden and hid underneath the willow tree; the branches were long and drooping and Brindle was completely hidden from view. Mrs Marsh came back to get her bag, but she did not notice that Brindle was not in the house. Then off she went to work.

Brindle sat under the tree quietly waiting. Very soon the door of Number 12 opened and Mr Tomkins walked down the garden path, through the garden gate and along the road to the bus stop. Brindle followed him, keeping out of sight, and while Mr Tomkins was waiting for the bus he hid behind the large leather briefcase of another man who was waiting there. Cairn Terriers are very small dogs and nobody noticed him.

Along came the bus, the long queue of people all crowded forward and climbed aboard, and Brindle slipped on unnoticed and crept under one of the seats. He kept very still and watched carefully. When he saw Mr Tomkins stand up ready to get off the bus, he quietly and very quickly followed him, keeping out of sight, hiding behind trees and dodging between parked cars.

Mr Tomkins worked for the Post Office. He drove a small

red van and delivered parcels all round the villages. When he reached the depot he unlocked the door of his red van and put his lunchbox in the back before going into the sorting office to collect his deliveries. Brindle saw his chance and quickly jumped into the van by the back door which was open, and hid amongst some empty sacks.

Mr Tomkins and another postman loaded the van with parcels, but they did not notice Brindle who was crouching motionless under the sacks! Then Mr Tomkins climbed into the driver's seat and set off on his rounds.

There was a large box to be delivered to the garage, then a package for a lady who lived in a beautiful white house. Brindle watched Mr Tomkins knock on the doors and wait for the people to sign his pad to say that they had received their parcels. Then he decided what to do.

At the next stop he jumped out of the van when Mr Tomkins had collected the parcel. He was careful to ensure that Mr Tomkins did not see him. Then he waited for him to come back to the van and he jumped up and barked, pretending to be lost.

'Why, Brindle!' said Mr Tomkins. 'What are you doing here so far from home?' He recognised Brindle by the black mark on his ear and his name on the collar. Brindle barked and wagged his tail cheerfully.

'You had better come with me,' said Mr Tomkins. 'You must be lost.' And he lifted Brindle onto the front seat of the van. He even gave him one of his biscuits that he was saving for his lunch.

Brindle had a lovely day. He helped deliver a box of flowers to a lady who had a birthday. The box had a big blue bow on it and the lady patted Brindle on the head, smiled, and gave him a dog biscuit. He delivered a bag full of apples to another house, and a box with a large toy car to a little boy, who was jumping up and down with excitement as he waited for it to arrive.

Next they delivered to the High Street and Brindle became friends with a shopkeeper and a lady who was out shopping. He made so many new friends and he stayed with Mr Tomkins all day until he had finished delivering his parcels. Then together they waited for the bus to take them home. This time Brindle did not have to hide, Mr Tomkins carried him onto the bus and all the passengers petted and made a fuss of him.

Meanwhile, Rhona and Rob had arrived home from school. They called Brindle, but of course he did not come running up to them as he usually did. They called and called! Rob went looking all round the house. He searched under the beds in case Brindle was playing hide and seek, he looked in the cupboards, but he was nowhere to be seen. Rhona noticed a large bump under the covers on one of the beds, but it was only an old teddy bear. She decided to look outside, but of course he was not there. They even looked in the garden shed. They began to feel worried and wondered whether they would ever find him.

'We had better look outside,' said Rhona, and they decided to search the neighbourhood, but he was nowhere to be found. The children called and shouted his name, 'Brindle, Brindle, where are you?' and just as they were wondering whether they would ever find him, they suddenly heard a bark and Brindle came bounding along the road towards them. They were so glad to see him, they hugged and patted him and stroked him on his rough-haired back. Brindle was pleased to see them too. He jumped up, wagging his tail, and he tried to tell them all about his adventurous day.

Mr Tomkins told the children how he had found Brindle in another village. *He did not know that Brindle had followed him and hidden in the van*, and of course Brindle could not tell them! The children and Mrs Marsh were amazed. How had Brindle managed to travel so far all by himself? *How had he got out of the house?* They wondered and wondered, but they did not find out.

The Marsh family were very glad to have Brindle home again, but they never did discover that he had followed Mr Tomkins. They just made a big fuss of him and wondered how he had managed to get out on his own?

Brindle and Mr Tomkins became special friends and Brindle would sometimes go for walks with him round the village. But he thought he had better not follow him to work again ... not for a while, anyway!

Sports Day

For the next few days the family made sure that Brindle was safely in the house when they set off each morning. They did not want him to get lost again!

Brindle sat by the window feeling very lonely and very sorry for himself. He watched Mr Tomkins going to work and wished that he could help him deliver the parcels in the little red van.

Next door at Number 8 lived the Harris family. Mr and Mrs Harris were both teachers. Mr Harris worked at the Technical College and Mrs Harris was a teacher at the school in the village where Rob and Rhona attended. Brindle watched them go to work too.

One Wednesday morning Rob and Rhona were very excited. It was Sports Day at school. They both wore their athletic kits when they set off in the morning and

waved goobye to Brindle. Brindle decided that he wanted to watch them race. *But how was he going to get out of the house and go to school?* He thought and thought, and then he had an idea... *But he would have to be extremely careful.*

When Mrs Marsh went into the garage, Brindle followed her. He was going to hide in the recycling box! He found a large paper bag inside the box and crept inside it. Wednesday was collection day. When Mrs Marsh carried the box out of the garage and put it by the front gate, she did not notice Brindle hiding inside the paper bag. He stayed in the box, keeping quite still so that no one would find him.

As soon as Mrs Marsh had driven to the estate agents, Brindle climbed out of the recycling box and trotted quietly along the road towards the school. When he arrived at Meadow Park School, the gates were tightly closed and securely locked, but Brindle was so small that he managed to squeeze underneath. Then he quickly ran over to the sports field where the chairs were already set out for the parents to watch the races. He decided to hide under a table where the judges were going to sit. It was covered with a green cloth that reached to the ground. Brindle was completely hidden from view, but if he lifted the edge of the cloth with his nose he could see the track clearly. Dogs were not allowed on the school field, so he sat very still until the children came out and the races began.

Soon the judges came and sat at the table. One of the lady judges was Mrs. Harris and she trod on the tip of Brindle's tail and he almost yelped, but he managed to remain quiet. He wanted to see Rob and Rhona racing.

The first event was the running race. Brindle watched, peeping out very carefully from under the green tablecloth. There were two races, then at last it was Rob's turn. He lined up at the start and when the whistle blew he ran as fast as he could to the finishing line. Brindle was so excited that he could not remain silent any longer. He dashed out and ran fast across the field, looking like a small furry football. He jumped up at Rob, who had come second. Rob was very surprised.

'Brindle!' he said. 'What are you doing here?'

Brindle jumped and barked excitedly, but then he thought he should stay hidden for a while longer. There were lots more races and he wanted to watch Rhona. So he quickly disappeared, dodging through the legs of the people and in and out of the chairs until he managed to creep unseen back under the table. He was so quick that in the confusion not one person saw where he had gone, and eventually the races started again.

The egg and spoon race was next. Rhona was very good at balancing the potato on the spoon. They did not use real eggs; it would have been very messy! She walked very carefully and quite quickly and soon she passed all the others, who had dropped their potatoes. Rhona came first and was given a red ribbon. She was very pleased. Brindle wanted to join in and he chased after one of the potatoes, picked it up in his mouth and ran to the winning post. He hoped he would get a red ribbon too! Everyone was most surprised, but Brindle ran off again and this time he crept under a lady's jacket to hide.

The best race was the obstacle course. The children had to climb through hoops, then balance on a bench without falling, jump in a sack and finally wriggle under a tarpaulin before they reached the winning post.

When Brindle saw Rob, he was so excited that he forgot to stay hidden. With a bark of excitement he ran and

jumped through a hoop! This was a race he could really enjoy! He ran along the bench and then jumped into the sack with Rob as he hopped along! Then he raced towards the tarpaulin. There were two boys wriggling under-neath and Brindle joined them. The parents and children laughed and cheered as he came out on the other side. Then he ran and chased, jumping up at Rob as he ran to the finishing line.

This time Brindle could not run away and hide. Rob held him firmly and they watched Rhona run in the obstacle race. At the end of Sports Day Brindle was awarded a special white rosette for the best dog in the obstacle race and Mrs. Harris attached it to his collar. Everyone clapped and cheered!

Once again the Marsh family could not discover how Brindle had managed to get out of the house. They checked every door and window when they arrived home, but they were all locked. It was a mystery! And of course Brindle did not tell them. After all, he might want to go out again on another recycling Wednesday.

Burglars!

Number 14, Green Trees Avenue was empty. It was the house next door to Mr Tomkins and nobody had lived there for several months.

One day Mrs Marsh came home from the estate agents and announced that they were going to have new neighbours. The empty house had been sold. Rob and Rhona were very excited because there were two children in the new family. They hoped they would have new friends. Brindle wondered whether there would be a dog to play with?

A few weeks later a large moving truck drew up at the empty house. Two men climbed out of the driving compartment and attached a wooden ramp to the back of the truck. Brindle watched them through the window with great interest and the men began unloading the furniture and boxes into the house. Soon a large grey car drove up and stopped outside number 14. A lady went in through the front door of the empty house. She was telling the men where to place the furniture.

Suddenly Brindle noticed an old van parked close by. Two rather shabby men climbed out and while the moving men were in the house they quickly and very quietly crept into the moving van. Then, looking all around them, they swiftly carried two boxes out and hurried back to their own van with them.

The moving men came out of the house to get more furniture. After they had unloaded a table and some chairs into the house, the two burglars came creeping back and took another box and a rug, which they quickly loaded into their van.

'Robbers!' thought Brindle, as he watched through the window and he wondered what to do? He started to bark, but no one could hear him. Suddenly he had an idea. *Maybe Mrs Marsh had forgotten to close all the windows.* He ran upstairs and looked in the bedrooms and the bathroom, but the windows were all closed. Then he went back downstairs and looked in the kitchen ... and yes, the window was open just a little at the top! This gave him an idea.

Brindle jumped onto a chair, then he crouched and sprang with an enormous leap from the chair into the sink. Fortunately there were no dirty dishes in it but it was rather wet and slippery. Next he climbed onto the draining board, where there were several plates drying.

Brindle stretched up on his back legs and he was just able to reach the window sill. He concentrated and squatted on his back legs then jumped as high as he could and just managed to land on the window sill. It was very narrow and Brindle's tail brushed against one of the plates. It fell with a crash to the floor and smashed into pieces!

'Oh dear!' thought Brindle. But he wanted to help catch those robbers, so he stretched up and reached the open window. He squeezed and squeezed and squeezed! The gap was very narrow. Then he gave the window latch a nudge with his nose and it opened a little more, and at last he was able to climb out.

He made an enormous jump down onto the red and white geraniums that were growing underneath the kitchen window. One of them was squashed when he landed! But Brindle did not wait around, he ran as fast as he could, jumping over the garden wall, and he raced along Green Trees Avenue until he came to the moving van. The robbers were trying to steal two more boxes. They were standing at the top of the ramp when Brindle arrived. He started to bark as loudly as he could, then he growled fiercly at the two burglars. The moving men and the lady came running out of the house to see what all the noise was about. The two burglars could not get away, as Brindle was snapping and biting at their legs. The men were very angry and shouted, 'Go away!' Brindle was angry too and growled ferociously at them.

When the lady and the moving men came outside and saw Brindle barking and growling at the robbers, they quickly phoned the police. At that moment Mr Tomkins came along and all of them, together with Brindle barking and snapping, managed to stop the burglars escaping. Then Mr. Tomkins decided to make a big slash in one of the van's tyres which meant the burglars could not drive away. When the police arrived they put the robbers in the police car. Brindle ran over to the old van to show them where the missing boxes were. The lady was very pleased and they all made a fuss of Brindle.

It was now just past three fifteen and Rob and Rhona were coming home from school. As they were walking along Green Trees Avenue they saw the police car and wondered what was happening? Then they saw Brindle and they ran towards the moving van to catch him.

'What is he doing outside by himself again?' they wondered.

Mrs Singh, the lady from the empty house, explained to them how Brindle had caught the burglars. They were very proud of him. Mrs Singh took Brindle's photograph and sent it to the newspaper. The next week there was a picture of him and a headline that said, 'BRINDLE CATCHES THE THIEVES'.

The Marsh family were very happy. They all wondered how Brindle had managed to get out of the house. They even looked at the kitchen window, but they did not think it was a wide enough gap for Brindle to get through and they certainly did not think he would be able to jump onto the window sill. Brindle did not show them how he had jumped from the chair to the sink and then onto the draining board. Neither did he show them how he had wiggled the window latch with his nose! After all, he might have to get out and catch burglars another day!

They all looked at the smashed plate and they thought that Brindle might have broken it, but they were not cross because he had caught the robbers. The next day, though, they closed the window, just in case, even though the gap was too small for Brindle. They all knew that he was a very clever dog.

Mr and Mrs Singh and their family moved in and Rob and Rhona soon had two new friends. Brindle was not quite so happy as the Singhs had a large tabby cat called Mouser. He was bigger than Brindle, so Brindle did not go visiting with Rob and Rhona. Mouser did not like dogs!

A Good Turn

Mr Marsh liked playing golf. When he came home from the golf club he would sit in the armchair and tell the family about his game. He usually played with his friend from the office, Mr Entwistle. Sometimes he would be sad because it took him so many strokes to get the golf ball into the hole.

Brindle did not really understand golf, but he did know that Mr Marsh would like to get a hole with one stroke. But he never did.

Brindle decided to help him. When Mr Marsh went to the golf club one Saturday, Brindle decided to go as well. He crept out when the garage was open and slipped behind the long drooping branches of the willow tree in the front garden. He had hidden there once before, when he had helped Mr Tomkins deliver the parcels.

Nobody could see him because the branches reached to the ground.

When Mr Marsh drove the car out of the garage and headed along Green Trees Avenue, Brindle slipped out and raced along the road, taking care that none of the family saw him. It was not far to the golf club. He headed for Meadow Park School and quickly squeezed under the school gates. Then he raced across the sports field and went creeping along the edge of the field until he found a small hole in the fence. It was just big enough and he squeezed and forced himself through.

He was on the golf course at last, close to hole Number 3, and nobody had seen him!

Mr Marsh and his friend were just starting to play the first hole, when Brindle crept along, hiding in the long grass and bushes. It was all very damp and muddy as it had been raining the day before. He watched them hit their golf balls towards the first hole. He did not want them to see him so he watched very quietly without moving.

Poor Mr Marsh had to hit the ball six times before it went into the first hole. Mr Entwistle managed it in three strokes. It was not any better at the second hole. Mr Marsh hit his ball into a large bunker. It took three hits to get it out close to the second flag. Altogether that was five strokes.

'Oh dear!' said Mr Marsh. 'Bother, bother, bother!' He was not happy. Mr Entwistle managed to get his ball in the hole with only four strokes. He was feeling pleased

with himself. Poor Mr Marsh!

Brindle decided that something had to be done.

He ran quickly to the next hole, dodging behind trees and brambles, making sure that Mr Marsh and Mr Entwistle did not discover him.

Mr Marsh lifted his golf club and hit the ball. It soared high in the air and almost hit a seagull that was flying by. The seagull squawked loudly and flew away. The golf ball landed in some bushes quite a long way from the third hole. It was going to be very difficult for Mr Marsh to hit the ball out of the long grass by the bushes.

In a trice Brindle raced over to the bushes and scrabbled and searched until he found the golf ball. Then, with a quick look behind him to make sure that he was not seen, he picked it up in his mouth and scampered as fast as he could to hole Number 3. He dropped the small white ball in the hole and raced off as fast as he could to hide.

Several minutes later Mr Marsh and Mr Entwistle came striding across the golf course and approached the third hole. They started looking for their golf balls; Mr Entwistle found his on the edge of the green, but Mr Marsh was still searching close to the bushes when Mr Entwistle shouted in great excitement.

'Your golf ball is in the hole!' he exclaimed. 'You've got a hole in one!'

Mr Marsh was overjoyed. When the other golfers heard, they all came over and congratulated him! Then they all went back to the golf club for a celebration party. A hole in one was very special. Mr Marsh was a champion!

Brindle thought he had better go home as quickly as he could. He hoped that nobody would see him. He wriggled through the hole in the fence and raced across the field to the school gate. Then he chased back along Green Trees Avenue until he reached home. He did not want anyone to know he had been out, so he crept under the willow tree to hide again.

It was not long before the children were calling him. When he came out from under the branches of the willow tree the children thought he had been having a nap! They did not know he had been to the golf club.

When Mr Marsh came home, he told everyone about his 'hole in one'. The family were pleased and very excited. Mr Marsh was very happy!

Brindle was so glad to see him happy that he jumped up and down and almost did a dance on his hind legs. How the family laughed!

Dogs were not allowed at the golf club, so Brindle decided not to go back, although he would have liked to have made another hole in one. But he never did. And neither did Mr Marsh!

Brindle Goes to Town

Every morning from Monday to Friday Mr Marsh went to work in the city, he would walk along Green Trees Avenue and then along the High Street to the station. The train came along at 8.10 a.m. The children would watch it gather speed and race along the rails and over the railway bridge on its way to town. They could see it through the living room window, or as they walked along the road to school. Brindle watched too and he wondered what it would be like to travel on a train.

He hoped that Mr Marsh would take him to the city, but whenever he jumped up and asked him Mr Marsh always said 'No!' very firmly.

One day, however, Mr Marsh announced that he was taking a later train as he had to go to a meeting. Brindle pricked up his ears and listened. Maybe this was his chance! And so he decided to go with him. Of course Mr Marsh did not know that Brindle was planning to escape again!

Once again he camouflaged himself amongst the coats in the hall. When Mrs Marsh went to get the car from the garage, he quickly slipped out and hid beneath the long trailing branches of the willow tree. Mrs Marsh did not notice that he was not in the house and she drove to work.

Brindle was very excited. He was free again! He thought for a while and then he decided to go to the station and wait for Mr Marsh there. So he slipped out from under the willow tree and slithered on his little brown stomach under the garden gate. Then he scampered along the road, dodging behind the parked cars until he came to the High Street. He had to be careful here because there were a lot of people walking along and he did not want to be seen.

So when he saw a very large lady with a long grey coat he crept very close and hid between her shopping bag and the coat. It was a very big shopping bag and a very long coat! Brindle hoped she would not notice him. Perhaps people would think he was on a leash.

The lady headed towards the station. Brindle followed her, taking great care not to bump into her legs, and she went into the ticket hall. Brindle looked for somewhere to hide as he wanted to wait for Mr Marsh. Suddenly he noticed a large noticeboard standing close to the far wall. There was a sign which said, 'REFRESHMENTS, ICE

CREAMS AND NEWSPAPERS'. Brindle crept behind the sign and waited, several trains came along. They were very noisy and lots of people climbed aboard and some people got off. No one noticed Brindle hiding behind the board.

At last Mr Marsh came along. Brindle jumped up and wagged his tail, he was so glad to see him. He almost barked in excitement, but then just in time he remembered that he must be quiet. *He had to get on the train without being seen.*

Brindle had a plan. He noticed that there was a compartment at one end of all the trains where people stowed their bikes, buggies and boxes. He decided to sneak aboard the train in a baby carriage or a box. He watched very carefully and when he saw a lady carrying her baby and getting ready to load her buggy on the train, he waited until she was talking to the guard. Then he raced along the platform and quickly jumped into the empty buggy and hid under the baby blanket. The guard helped the lady to load it into the last compartment with all the bicycles and boxes.

Brindle was on the train! He was on his way. He felt very pleased with himself. But he decided to stay hidden for a while before he set off to find Mr Marsh.

The train trundled and rattled as it raced along the track and after a while it stopped at a station. Brindle peeped out through the open door of the train to see if Mr Marsh was getting off. There was no sign of him on the platform, so

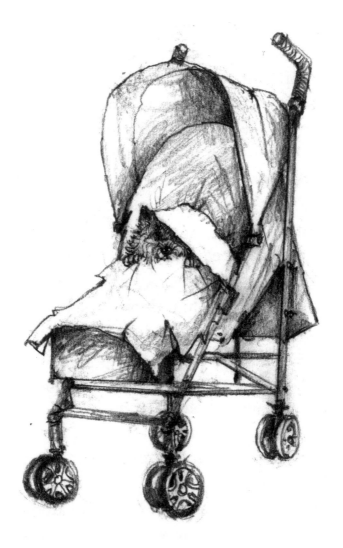

Brindle jumped back into the buggy and waited for the train to start. Soon it was jolting, bouncing and racing along the track. Brindle thought that he should start to search for Mr Marsh, as he wanted to be sure that he would get off at the same station. So when the guard came into the last compartment he peeked out from under the blanket to see if the door to the other carriages was open. It was! Brindle leaped out of the buggy, raced into the first carriage and quickly hid under a seat before anyone could see him.

It was not difficult to creep under the seats, although he had to be very careful not to bump into the legs of all the people who were travelling on the train. He even found a very tasty biscuit that someone had dropped! He was very tempted to pick up a small toy bear that he found under a seat, but he thought that the little boy on the seat might miss it.

At last in the second carriage he recognised Mr Marsh. He was wearing navy blue socks with red diamonds on them. He also recognised his black shoes with the laces that Brindle had chewed a few days before! He could not see the rest of him from under the seat, so he hid until they reached the station where Mr Marsh got off.

Brindle followed close behind him and when Mr Marsh was walking along the platform, he ran up to him and barked and jumped and rolled over. Mr Marsh did not notice him for a minute or so. But when he got to the ticket barrier the guard said, 'Is this your dog? He needs a ticket.' Mr Marsh looked down and there, sure enough, was Brindle! He could not believe his eyes. Mr Marsh bent down and picked Brindle up.

'How did you get here?' he asked.

Brindle just barked and barked in a friendly way. But Mr Marsh was not pleased. He bought a ticket for Brindle and then he carried him out to where a car was waiting for them. Fortunately the driver was amused. 'That's a very clever dog you have there!' he said.

The two men took Brindle to the meeting and everyone was amazed and wondered how such a small dog had found his way onto the train without being seen. Mr Marsh told them stories about Brindle's other adventures and soon he stopped being cross and was laughing with all of them. Mr Marsh had a very good meeting, and everyone was so friendly towards Brindle. He certainly was a remarkably adventurous dog, but he wondered what the children would say when they discovered that he was missing again!

After the meeting Mr Marsh telephoned Rob and Rhona so that they would not worry and then he set off to the station. On the way he bought some dog biscuits and a small bowl. Brindle had a drink of water on the train and nibbled some biscuits. Mr Marsh had to carry him because he did not have a leash.

When he got home, the whole family wondered and wondered how Brindle had managed to escape and travel on the train. Brindle tried to tell them, but of course they did not understand. He did not show them his hiding place under the willow tree though!

For the next few weeks they were very careful to check that he was at home when they left for work and school. As for Brindle, he did not think he would go on a train by himself again for a while. It was very crowded and noisy as it rattled along, and there were so many legs that he had to be careful not to bump into!

A Walk by the River

Sometimes Rob and Rhona's grandpa came to visit the Marsh family at Number 10 Green Trees Avenue. Brindle was always happy to see him because he usually stayed for two weeks; while he was visiting Brindle did not feel lonely when the family went to work and school. In the mornings Grandpa would take Brindle for a walk. They usually went along the road past the school towards the river. This was an exciting walk for Brindle; there were so many interesting things to see.

One Tuesday morning Grandpa decided he was going to walk along the riverbank and have a cup of tea at the restaurant, which was close to where the swans and ducks usually swam. He was going to do some fishing, so he collected a small folding stool and his fishing line. Brindle wanted to go with him. They walked along Green

Trees Avenue and on the way they met Mrs Tomkins. She was going shopping, but she stopped and chatted with Grandpa, telling him all about Brindle's adventures with Mr Tomkins and how Brindle had helped him deliver the parcels. Grandpa laughed and chuckled and then they went on their way until they arrived at the path which led down to the riverbank.

The trail was muddy because it had been raining during the night, so Grandpa walked carefully until they reached the towpath that went along beside the river. Brindle ran beside him and soon they came to a very large oak tree that grew close to the riverbank. Grandpa sat down on his folding stool underneath the long spreading branches and started fishing. Brindle was allowed to wander around amongst the ferns and weeds; he loved to look in the river and search along the bank for small animals. Sometimes he would see a frog and once he had seen a water rat, but he did not manage to catch it. The river had quite fast-flowing water, so Brindle did not go swimming. He liked to wade in, where the water was shallow and where there were large rocks that he could climb on. When he stood on the rocks he would bark at the ducks and watch the swans swimming past. Then he would gaze at the gulls that searched and dived for fish as they flew squawking above the water.

After about an hour Grandpa packed up his fishing gear and they walked further along the bank to the res-taurant. It was called The Fisherman's Rest. Grandpa sat at a table by the side of the river and he enjoyed his cup of tea and biscuits. Brindle had some biscuits too. They watched the rowing boats on the river and chatted to a man who was fishing close by. Then after a while they headed back along the riverbank towards home. The path was very slippery in places and Grandpa had to be very careful not to slide as he carried his fishing rod and folding stool. It was a beautiful sunny day and it was not long before they reached the track that led back to the road. As they climbed up the slope they came to some large rugged boulders that were in the way. They stepped carefully over them but Grandpa's fishing rod became tangled in the branches of an overhanging tree. He stopped and tried to pull it free. He pulled and tugged, but the line had become caught in some brambles. Grandpa pulled harder. His foot slipped and he fell down, twisting his leg as he landed in the muddy earth beside the rocks. Brindle looked very anxiously to see if he had been hurt.

Grandpa could not get up and Brindle was very worried. He looked up at him, then he wagged his tail and barked. He was trying to tell Grandpa that he would go and get some help.

Poor Grandpa, his leg was hurting and it was a very lonely path. Very few people came along during the week, when all the children were at school and the grown-ups had gone to work. He thought that he might have to wait a long time before someone came along. His leg was very painful.

Suddenly he had an idea. He took his diary out of his pocket and wrote on an empty page:

I have fallen down and hurt my leg. I am on the path by the river. Please get help.

Next he took a shoelace from one of his shoes and tied the note and the shoelace to Brindle's collar and he said urgently, 'Go and get help, Brindle!'

Brindle barked three times and set off up the path towards the road. He ran as fast as his short legs would go, and when he came to the road he decided to head towards the village where Mrs Marsh worked. He jumped and turned and ran very quickly. When he came to the estate agents he was very pleased to see that her car was outside, which meant that Mrs Marsh was there and was not visiting any houses. He ran to the door and barked as loudly as he could.

Mrs Marsh was not pleased when she saw Brindle. She thought that he had escaped again! She got up from her desk and came and opened the door. Brindle barked excitedly and jumped up to show her the note.

When Mrs Marsh read the note she said, 'Well done, Brindle!' Then she walked quickly back to her desk and dialled 999.

It was not long before an ambulance was on its way. Mrs Marsh picked Brindle up and took him in the car. Then together they went back to the path that led down to the river. Grandpa was very pleased to see them. His leg was still very painful. 'Good dog, Brindle!' he said.

Soon the ambulance arrived, it stopped on the road and two paramedics came along the path with a stretcher. They very carefully picked Grandpa up and helped him to lie on the stretcher. Then they covered him with a blanket and strapped him securely so that he would not roll off. One of the men, whose name was Luke, said he thought that Grandpa had broken a bone in his leg. They had to carry him very carefully along the bumpy, slippery path. But in a few minutes they were back on the road and Grandpa was put in the ambulance and taken to hospital. The paramedics were very impressed when they heard how Brindle had managed to get help.

Mrs Marsh took Brindle home, then she drove to the hospital to see how Grandpa was getting on.

'Dogs are not allowed in hospitals,' explained the ambulance men. Brindle was very disappointed. He had always wondered what it was like inside a hospital and he wanted to see that Grandpa was getting help with his leg.

When the children came home from school and Mr Marsh came back from work, they were most concerned and worried. They hoped that Grandpa's leg would heal soon. They were all very pleased and proud of Brindle. If he had not run off with the note, it might have been several hours before anyone would have come along and helped him. Brindle was patted and praised, and they said that he was a very clever dog. But he was not allowed to visit Grandpa, who had to stay in hospital for several days.

Brindle was worried, and he decided that he wanted to see how Grandpa was getting on in hospital. Gradually a plan came into his mind. He thought and thought and thought, but he could not do anything until the next day. *Of course, he did not tell the family his plan.*

Visiting the Hospital

The next day was Wednesday and Brindle was very happy, he was hoping to hide in the recycling box again! Then he thought that he would be able to go and see Grandpa. After the children had gone to school and Mr Marsh had left to go to the station, Brindle crept into the garage. He had found a large carrier bag in the kitchen and carried it in his mouth into the garage. He dropped it in the recycling box and then climbed inside it and hid amongst the newspapers and magazines.

It was not long before Mrs Marsh came into the garage. She picked up the recycling box and carried it to the garden gate. As soon as she had left to go to work, Brindle peeped out of the bag and when no one was coming he jumped out and headed down the road towards the High Street.

He knew that ambulances often came along the High Street on their way to the hospital, and he decided to follow one. The High Street was very busy; workmen were drilling a large hole in the road as they were installing new cables for electricity. Brindle did not like the noise of the drills and he rushed past as fast as he could. He hurried along past the supermarket and almost jumped on a bus, but he was not sure that it was going the right way. Then, just ahead of him outside the old people's retirement home, he noticed an ambulance waiting. It had come to take some people to the hospital.

Brindle stopped and hid behind a parked lorry. He watched the paramedics go into the old people's home and then he crept cautiously into the ambulance. He knew where to hide, and found a place under the bed where the paramedics had put Grandpa's stretcher. Soon two ladies came out of the retirement home and climbed into the ambulance. One had her arm in a plaster and the other lady was going to have physiotherapy for a stiff back. They sat down and the paramedics closed the door. Soon they were on their way. Brindle was very pleased to leave the bustle and noise of the town. He did not like the rushing traffic in the High Street and he especially did not like the noise of the pneumatic drills as they bored into the pavement.

The ambulance was a very interesting vehicle. Brindle wondered what all the tubes and bottles and medical equipment were for. But he did not have time to find out, as very soon they arrived at the hospital. The ambulance stopped and the ladies stepped out, Brindle crept out too and hid behind a litter bin where he could see the ambulances arriving. He watched for a while and then he decided to go into the Accident and Emergency Department. There were lots of people there with hurt legs and arms and he thought he might find Grandpa, so he slipped quietly through the doors.

A man with a big plaster on his leg was waiting on a trolley. Brindle thought he might be going to the same ward as Grandpa. He looked very carefully around and then he jumped onto a bench and, when no one was looking, he jumped onto the trolley and crept under a

blanket. He stayed very still. As he was such a small dog, nobody noticed the bump under the blanket at the end of the trolley. He was very careful not to bump into the man.

Two men in white coats came along. They started to wheel the trolley along a long corridor. The man lying on the trolley was called Mr Brown. They went into a lift and soon they were going up to the third floor. Mr Brown was going into the Orthopaedic Ward. Brindle peeped out from under the blanket. There were lots of beds with men who had broken legs and arms. They all had plasters or special coverings over them.

Suddenly Brindle saw Grandpa at the far end of the ward. He crept out from under the blanket, jumped down from the trolley and ran across the ward. He gave a happy bark, climbed onto a chair and then leaped onto Grandpa's bed. Grandpa was very surprised. He said, 'Why, Brindle! What are you doing here?'

The doctors and nurses all came running over to Grandpa's bed. 'Where did he come from?' they wondered. They were not pleased, because dogs were not allowed in the hospital.

Grandpa told them all how Brindle had fetched help when he had hurt his leg.

They stopped being so cross and one of them said, 'I expect he wanted to see how you are!' Then they all laughed.

But Brindle could not stay in the ward and the nurse

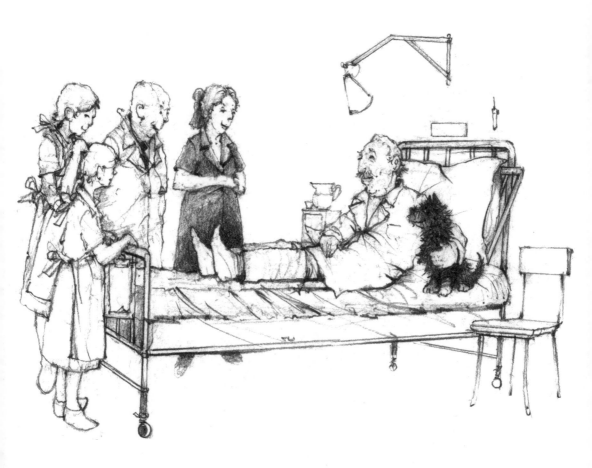

telephoned Mrs Marsh. Brindle barked goodbye to Grandpa and he went home with Mrs Marsh. Once again the family were very surprised and wondered how he had escaped from the house.

Grandpa came home in a few days. He had to use crutches, so they could not go for walks, but they did enjoy sitting in the garden. Brindle decided that he had better not escape for a while, the family were checking very carefully to see that he was safely indoors when they went to school and work. They had not been pleased when he had found his way to the hospital, although they were very glad that he had wanted to see that Grandpa was getting well. Brindle was happy too. He had been to the hospital and he had travelled in an ambulance.

But best of all, he had helped Grandpa.

THE END